IN MOMMY'S CLOUD

(AN INTRODUCTION TO CLOUD COMPUTING)

WRITTEN BY LILIAN SHULIKA TATA

ILLUSTRATED BY SONA & JACOB

EDITED BY LAWIR MUHAMMED

Written by Lilian Shulika Tata
Illustrations by Sona and Jacob
Edited by Lawir Muhammed

Edition I Edition 2022

ISBN 979-8-9874710-1-2

Dedication

This book is dedicated to our
most precious and adorable daughters
who inspired this, Haneefa and Faizah;
to their amazing cousins Lael and Talia,
and to every kid out there,
you are loved.
May your curiosity keep growing.

Hanee and Fifi lived in a beautiful street called Blue Heron with their mom and dad. Their cousins, Lael and Talia, played with them a lot.

They all heard Mom and Dad talk about "the cloud" and teach on it daily. They thought it was the clouds in the sky.

One sunny day, after hearing so much about the cloud, Hanee asked, "Mommy, Mommy, can I go to your cloud?"

"Sure, my love, I'll take you to my cloud," Mommy replied with a surprised look on her face.

"Mommy, is your cloud in the playground?"
Hanee's sister, Fifi, asked.

Little did Mommy think of the cloud as a
playground. So, Mommy said, "Yes, pumpkin,
my cloud is a playground."

Hanee was eager to know what was in
Mommy's playground, so, she asked,
"Mommy, do you have slides in your
playground?"

"Yes baby, I have so many slides. Huumm, I have an idea... How about I tell you a story of Mommy's cloud playground?" Mommy replied.

"Yaay Yaay, we wanna hear it," they responded. "Story... story... story..." they sang while hitting the table.

That day, they had a playdate
with their cousins.
So, Hanee, Fifi, Lael, and Talia
quickly sat around Mommy to
hear this story.

Mommy told them this story...

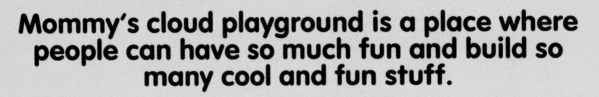

Mommy's cloud playground is a place where people can have so much fun and build so many cool and fun stuff.

In Mommy's cloud playground, there are different clouds.
There's Cloud Amazon, Cloud Azure, Cloud Google and other clouds.
Each playground has different activities.

To get into mummy's cloud playground, you go through a big Gateway. And you need mommy's permission to get in.

Inside the cloud playground, there are many play stations. At each play station, there is a security guard to protect your game. He will let your friend play with you if you grant them permission.

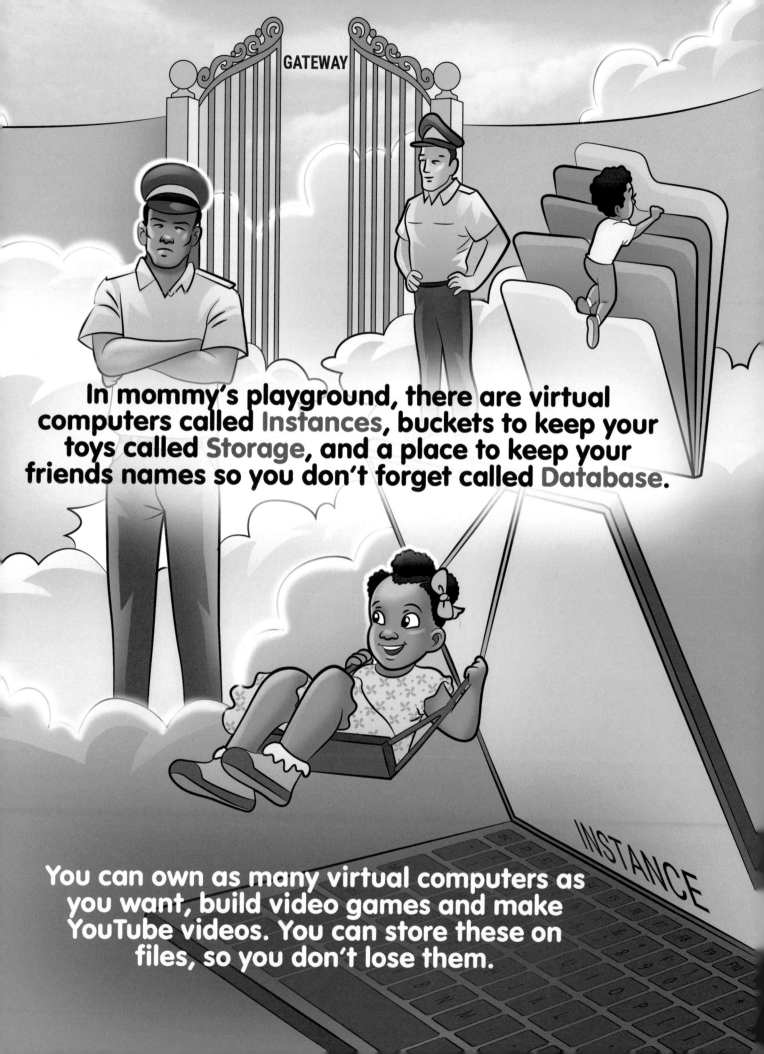

GATEWAY

In mommy's playground, there are virtual computers called Instances, buckets to keep your toys called Storage, and a place to keep your friends names so you don't forget called Database.

You can own as many virtual computers as you want, build video games and make YouTube videos. You can store these on files, so you don't lose them.

INSTANCE

Do you know you can build your own private cloud and protect it from the bad guys with a big Firewall?

There are buckets where you can store your toys, books, and pictures. You can also share these with your friends secretly.

There is a playroom where you can keep and hide all your information like your friends' names so you don't forget called Database.

In Mommy's cloud, you can build a robot. Alexa and Siri can be your cloud robot friends. Ask them any question you want.

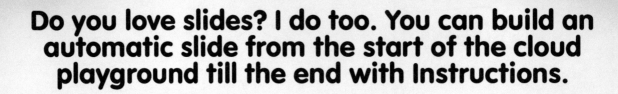

Do you love slides? I do too. You can build an automatic slide from the start of the cloud playground till the end with Instructions.

Then Hanee asked, "Mommy, what if I fall and get a booboo?"

"Oh, don't worry sweetheart, there are cloud doctors called Engineers who will take care of your booboo and make sure you are strong again," Mommy answered.

Then Mommy continued...

Oh, Do you know you can work in the cloud?
In Mommy's cloud, you can build anything you
want, big or small, and you can dream
whatever you want.

In Mommy's cloud, the possibilities are endless.
Do you want to build your playground in
mommy's cloud?

"Let's start, what do you want to call it?"

"Hummmmm," they shouted together...
Daddy cloud..., Hanee Cloud..., Fifi cloud...,
Mommy cloud...

And then they started singing...

Mommy cloud dudu dudu dudu
Mommy cloud dudu dudu dudu
Daddy cloud dudu dudu dudu... dudu dudu dudu

What do you want your cloud to be called...?

And that was how this became their favorite bedtime story.

Glossary

Cloud computing - Cloud computing in simple terms is the ability for companies to rent and use computers, storage and networks over the internet without spending millions of dollars in purchasing, setting up and maintaining equipment. They have the flexibility to rent as much or as little as they need at any moment. This helps them save costs enormously and focus on growing the business.

This has made it possible for even small business needing IT infrastructure to be easily setup with so little upfront capital.

Instances - An instance is a virtual server or virtual computer in the cloud that can perform computations like your computer, but without the physical component. You can rent a virtual computer and run your workloads in the cloud.

Storage - Cloud storage allows cloud users to be able to store object data like pictures and files. Think of a hard drive or memory card. What you can store on your hard drive, you can store in cloud storage (pictures, word, pdf, video files etc). Today, most people use google photos to store pictures in the cloud, Dropbox other examples.

Database - A database is an organized collection of information that is stored in a computer. For example: student registration information, students grades in an exams, patients information in a hospital

Gateway - Gateway is the bridge between your services in the cloud and the rest of the world. It literally is a gate controlling flow of information into and out of the cloud. Just like a school gate through which authorized personnel go in and out; the cloud gateway serves the same purpose.

WAF - Web Application Firewall is a cloud armor that protects your applications from the bad guys. It helps monitor any malicious incoming internet traffic and blocks them from accessing your applications.

Just imagine building a firewall around your house, how many people will get in, except you open up one part and explicitly allow certain people in. That is what WAF does.

About the author

Lilian Shulika Tata was born in the Northwest Region of Cameroon, Nso, and a mother of 2 very precious girls who inspired the book. She holds 3 master's degrees. She's currently completing her Ph.D. thesis in Information technology.
She has carried out quite a few research projects and blogs about technology and careers in tech. She started her career as a Diplomat, but her research led her to the world of technology, where she is now settled on Cloud Technologies and uses her knowledge to volunteer and teach students.
She is passionate about family, education, technology, and Artificial intelligence. A very creative and adventurous person, always eager to learn and share her knowledge with the world.

www.shulikatata.com

This story was inspired by true life events with our daughters Haneefa A.S. Lawir (4 years old) and Faizah A.L. Lawir (2 years old). Having heard their parents talk a lot about the cloud, they wanted to be part of it. Unfortunately, it will not be the cloud they know.

One day, she reaches out to mommy, and she asked if she could go to mummy's cloud, so mommy says yes, and her sister asked if it is a playground. The questions kept coming and we had to figure out a way to tell them a story about the cloud. We made up a story and told them. Later that night, after reading their bedtime story, Haneefa wanted to hear Mommy's cloud story, So Lawir and I had to find a way of telling them cloud stories. This is how In Mommy's Cloud was born, it became their favorite bedtime story. We decided to document it for them, and eventually, it became a project where we thought to introduce them to all the terms and resources, and technology in the form of a storybook. Well, here we are today.

Their curiosity led to this beautiful story which will be followed by other concepts in the domain of Cloud Computing, and more in the field of technology.

We do hope it creates the Value intended.

Made in the USA
Columbia, SC
13 September 2024

42105543R00018